This book is dedicated to the memory of

Randy Losh

Patty Maze

& Jim McCall

Words can't describe how much you all meant to me; I miss you every day. Thank you all for your kindness, love, motivation and constant support for my dreams. The world has been a bit darker since you all left.

"The Light at the Edge of the Dock"

It all started in a child's mind. Visions of an empty void. He would search for his destination for years and always come up short. The dreams would haunt his very being, even as he aged. It came to him in a dream, when he was only seven years old. It was a bleak spring morning in April. He arose from the fields as the sun was starting to flare up the hills behind him. These hallucinations would always revisit him, every four years like a recurring illness, a curse upon his mental stability. The more and more he explored these hills the path became clearer. The fog surrounding him brought him eternal comfort. A sense of nirvana took over his thoughts. As he walked through the dew-covered grass, he always felt a presence with him. A presence that was quite unsettling, but he knew it would never harm him. He could feel the wind brush up against his body as if the ground beneath him was moving like the ocean waves.

Every time he would come back to this world, he got closer and closer to the truth. The lack of common noise confused his sense of direction. As the mountain and trees were speaking to him, he knew that there was a stronger force guiding him through this majestic wasteland. He could feel the rugged rocks beneath his feet as he walked down the trail leading to the outer rim of the fields. The boy could not see, because of the light at the bottom of the hill. As he got closer and closer in every dream, the fog would clear. The noises would be drowned out by the sound of rushing water. He is twenty-one now, and the visions have gotten stronger. He knew in his heart that this would be the final stance; all the signs that haunted him for years have finally started to make sense. As he laid his head down on his pillow, he started to feel his problems slipping away from him. He awakes in the fields that have welcomed him time and time again. This phenomenon became his second home. A place to escape from reality. As he started to walk the trail that he had been down a million times before he could feel the world around him start to shake. There was a change in the air, the trees have started to die, and the grass has started to rot away with every step. As he pulled closer to the outer rim of the fields, the fog revealed a dock. A place he has seen before but has never actually been able to reach. The wind is whistling through his ears as the sun starts to rise. He can feel some type of entity pulling him towards the dock. He welcomed it with open arms, believing that he has been waiting his whole life for this moment.

As he puts his feet on the dock, the cold, damp wood makes his knees tremble. He can see the world around him getting brighter as the dock itself keeps getting longer. The sounds of the world have stopped; all that is left is the rocking of the dock and the water in motion. The feeling of satisfaction takes over his mind as he reaches the edge of the dock. The pounding in his heart could be heard throughout the entire world. His fingers are shaking, as he gets on his knees. His legs feel so heavy; his lips start to become numb of the anticipation for coming events. As he leans over the edge of the dock the light begins to dim. He sees the blooming weeds and fish swimming about the chilling water. A tiny whirlpool begins to reveal something hidden at the bottom of the lake. A book graces the surface of the depths with a flash of light. The voices were deafening as he stared into the water, his body seemed to be floating as he reached out for the book. Overwhelmed by the powerful vibrations around him, it seemed like the book was farther and farther away. As his head and arm were slowly being engulfed by the water around him, he could see the book open.

When the book turned its pages, it was revealing to him everything he ever wanted. The truth that laid behind the messages, the dreams. As the book's presence was dragging him closer and closer to the bottom of the lake. He became a fabric amongst the wildlife in the water. The voices in the water were becoming a never-ending agitation; the underwater world around him became dark. As he finally gets his hands on the book. He realizes that he is not alone. As he struggled to swim back to the top of the water the earth was shaking, the water around him was shattering like glass. Every inch of his being was being pulled back further and further. He grows tired, his legs get weak. His lungs are filled with water and the dirt from the murky waters. Then he sees it, the presence that has been calling him there. The entity, which has always been so inviting to him over the years. It was pale and had the shape of a human. At first, he didn't know what to think, but it was something much more powerful than anything he could ever imagine.

As the entity got closer, and closer to him. He did not panic; he sat there in awe, welcoming whatever it might be hopefully to reveal his purpose there. The creature was getting bigger as it was approaching; it had bright green eyes like the fields once had when he was a child. The scales on the creature released all the noises he once heard. Screaming, and crying of children. The sounds of doctors and nurses blaring through the waters like a marching band. He could see paintings, and drawings. Hear nursery rhymes that used to fill his life with joy. As he was starting to fade away everything became white, and cold like the crisp winds on the fields. The creature stuck out his hand without saying a word. As they made eye contact, he could sense nothing but complete horror but an unusual sense of serenity. The walls are closing in; the creature begins to drag him to the docks. The world around him is nothing but flashes of light and crashing noises as he begins to lose consciousness. Fields became a long hallway, and the forests he once traveled in started to become filled with visions of wheelchairs and broken cabinets. Rocks beneath him have become broken syringes; his legs are covered in cuts from the path. He takes one last glance at the world around him and sees children skipping and playing in the yard. A butterfly lands on the window as a man bashes his head into the wall. With his final gust of wind left in his lungs he asks.

"What is this place?"

The creature turns around with a demeaning stare that could make mountains crumble.

"You are home my boy."

A silence takes over the room. As water spills from his mouth and his lungs start to collapse. His lips start to shake, and as his mind starts to fall apart, he stutters.

"Are you God?"

"No boy, we all are."

Then the door in this realm seals shut as the muttered screams of the world echo in his head. The last bit of light leaves his eyes as the window shuts, and the children stop singing. The final grip of his mentality was lost within his own mind. Strapped down to a chair, to lurk out at nighttime once everyone else was asleep. He was finally found inside the bathtub on the 4th floor. His lifeless body was curled up and molded to the steel around him. As death gripped its hands around the entire existence of his being. He finally found his purpose in this world and in others… to go back home, where he could live forever in the fields that once comforted a lonely child.

"The House Beyond the Forest"

The dirt road leading behind the town hall was filled with haunting stories and fantasies beyond comprehension. As the children play and sing on their way to school, they were always warned to never pass the rusted fence leading into the molded woods. The stories were passed down generation to generation. Even the thought of what lies beyond the woods would send chills down the spine of the families in Newpoint. The dry, dust filled air quickly turned into snow as the winter season creeped its way upon the mountains surrounding the town. That's when the noises started to become clearer. As the nights became darker, the streets became empty. The horrifying sounds would echo through the alleyways and corners of Newpoint.

On Christmas Eve some of the local children decided to investigate. Their common interests gave them the courage to finally pass through the very fence they were warned about growing up. As they were making their way through the forest it was as if time stood still. Snowflakes were frozen in place, like statues in the air. The children were in awe as they saw the crystal-clear ice cover the trees. Not aware of the horrors that lay ahead of them, they continued down the path. There was an old wooden bridge leading across the water. But they could not see the other side, as if it was just absent of any light. Even the moon disappeared behind its presence. They start to make their way across the bridge. Cautious it might fall apart; they took very slow and steady steps as the water beneath them started to roar in their ears. Once across, the children froze in place. Not aware of their surroundings, the natural sounds of the world started to fade. Complete silence took over the land in front of them. The snow was melting before their very eyes, ice melting as if the sun was hitting the Earth. Finally free from their frozen state, their sense of time became distant. As they traveled further the forest was turning into dirt. Cacti started to grow from the depths of the sand as scorpions ran past their feet.

The structure that appeared in the distance seemed to be lost as their vision became glossy. A house was sitting in the middle of the walkway. Surrounded by a swamp and boiling air. Not knowing where they were, or where they have ended up. They proceeded to walk up on the porch to see if anyone was home. All their minds were in a twist as their recent experiences have seemed to make them lose a grip on reality. One of the kids knocked on the door, as a bunch of scuffling echoed behind the rotten wood it slowly peered open. They walk in to see the house torn apart; old furniture laid in ruble and rotten food all over the kitchen.

Cockroaches covered most of the dinner table as the rotten smell rained through their noses. They decided to travel deeper into the house; with every step dust flew into the air. Water stained the walls around them as the sound of spiders weaving their webs echoed through the hallway. Some of the children went into the living room as the rest decided to venture upstairs. The fear of what could be lurking around every corner slowly seeped its way into their minds. The living room was filled with mold and torn pictures. Some of them have dates that go all the way back to the 18th century. The children were amazed by how much the house was damaged but somehow managed to still be standing after all these years. The children upstairs found a little girl's room, filled with dolls and open candy wrappers that have collected dust over the years. Peeking from the closet was a little light, and the sound of music. As they opened the door there was a music box with a diary underneath it. As they searched for a way to open it the ceiling started to crack. The noises from the attic stopped them in their tracks; the look of fear took over their faces as they were unaware of what could be in the house. The children hurried downstairs to show the others what they discovered but they seemed to have vanished. There was not a trace of them anywhere in the main hall. They all scattered trying to find their way out, but the house started to change. Doors became locked, the light from the outside started to become distant as they traveled further in the house.

They finally made it to the main hallway; a chill took over the air that surrounded them as they saw the glare of a fireplace behind the glass doors. As they walked through the room looked to be unharmed. The wood on the furniture was polished and the rug was as soft as the winter snow back home. As they proceeded into the room a rocking chair in front of the fire started to move. The music box from upstairs became louder with every step. The music was deafening as they got closer to the chair. As they started to turn, there was an old woman in the chair holding a doll. She was singing such a beautiful lullaby that put the children in a trance. Their bodies became solid as their knees started to get heavier. The woman turns and glares into their eyes. Their souls panicking as they fear there is no way out. With her rotten teeth and solid white eyes, she says.

"Are you here to play with me?"

"It's been a long time since my family has let me have friends over."

The children were in shock, not knowing how to react to their current state. As they finally regained their ability to move, they dashed out the door opening to find the way out. The woman screamed in terror as the children's sweat hit off the ground like a jackhammer on the concrete. Without warning, shadows started surrounding the children. As they make it to the front door, a sign of light has grasped their eyes. Then the diary opens, covering them in blood as the words melt from the pages. The final chapter of the diary became splattered on the wall. Crying and whimpering as their life pours from their bodies. The shadows begin to sing; another man appears from the corners of the shadows. As the woman they once saw was now just a little girl.

She ran to their legs, holding them as tight as she could and said "Don't be afraid. You're a part of the family now."

As the children scream in terror the shadows grab their feet and drag them back into the darkness that surrounds the hallway. The girl was singing as her father picked her up. The haunting melody would ring in their ears for what seemed like an eternity as he snapped her neck. Laughing diabolically at his deeds, he slams the door shut and his daughter's lifeless body turns into rotting flesh and a pile of maggots. The children were now lost in a world with no light. No sense of reality, the air became thinner as the shadows consumed the room around them. The sounds of laughter, and bickering filled the room as their lungs started to collapse. Water was starting to rise, and what strength they had left had vanished from their bodies.

The children were later found, frozen in the county lake. Set up like beautiful statues guarding the land around them. Ice peering from their eyes, and torn clothing. They were forever a part of the very lands that took their last breaths. Birds flocked around as the town became silent. Parents are forever haunted by the sights of their children's lifeless bodies. To never really know what happened to them, or what happened at the house that lay beyond the forest.

"Shark Tooth Tavern"

Off the shore of the Ancient Coves there was a tavern older than the Gods themselves. Tales of mighty warriors and legendary beasts haunted the streets leading to it. Only the bravest of adventures could dare enter such halls. There was a wall dedicated to all the famous captains that visited the tavern. The mead was the strongest in all the land, and the wench Muriel Scottdale owned the tavern for what seemed to be an eternity. Her crew was made up of all the youngest lasses in the harbor. There was word around town that she had a brothel upstairs in the tavern. Sailors from all the seven seas would visit the Shark Tooth Tavern. You would be lucky to even find a seat in the whole place.

One night during the celebration of Ole Tom's daughter Maggie's wedding, a loud screech was heard from the bowls of the ocean. A man that none of us have ever laid eyes on came crashing through the doors of the tavern. He warned us of the events to come, of an ancient creature that has been woken from its slumber. He told us tales of an ancient prophecy, one that cursed the land we celebrated upon. The wind started to howl, and the harbor started to shake as an unexpected storm rolled in. It covered every inch of the town. The mysterious old man went on to tell us a tale about an ancient being. An elder who lived in the depths below the harbor. The prophecy foretold of a celebration that would mark the start of the harvest waves. That the creature would awaken once someone of virgin blood sealed their fate in marriage. Maggie's eyes were drenched in tears as he continued to warn us all our future. Her husband, Dale Steelenge told the man to leave the tavern at once. Before he left, he warned us that someone among us was marked with the demon's curse.

As everyone was starting to settle down from the unexpected visitor it started to rain harder as the minutes passed us by. A member of my crew said he was going to tie our ship down to the dock before the storm got even worse. I sat there in a daze not ready for what would happen next. As he left the tavern, darkness came over the land. All we heard was the faint screams as he was being dragged away by an unseen force. Everyone in the tavern started to panic, the sailors and other crews started to barricade everyone in the tavern. As we all sat in terror there was a voice in the distance screaming for help. It was our crew mate; the 1st mate was trying to tear down the barricades. Begging and pleading that he was still alive. Once he got the door opened, we all witnessed a horror not known to the human eye. He was covered in cuts; his eyes were gone as he held out his hands. The scales on his flesh were releasing such an awful stench. As he lunged towards the door Ole tom shot him with his musket. The rest of the crews tried to rebuild the barricades on the door. I sat and watched as everyone seemed to be losing their minds over the events that just occurred. Maggie pointed out to everyone that Muriel was missing. We tried to search the Tavern, but the basement was locked so a group walked upstairs. As I go down to my last pint, we hear the howling of grown men being torn apart. The venture upstairs was unsettling as we saw the bodies scattered across the halls. It was such a sight that even the legendary Ching Shih couldn't have committed such acts. What was left of Muriel's crew was nothing but mutated abominations. Possessed succubus, feasting upon the flesh of the men. The quest from here was to lock them upstairs until we figured out how to slay the beasts. There were only a handful of us left alive after these attacks. Ole Tom was in the corner trying to comfort her as her husband and I devised a plan on how to survive this wretched night. Someone from my crew made it out alive from the attack of the she-devil. We opened the door and let him downstairs so Tom could aid his wounds. The night was becoming colder as the hours went on. Still no sign of Muriel, anywhere in the Tavern. Most of us just assumed she was dead until we heard a faint knock at the basement door. Tom and I tried to open the door but there was an old lock blocking our efforts. As we searched for the keys there was a muffled grunt coming from the front of the tavern. My crew mate was behind the bar, vomiting clear liquids. As I approached him you could see his skin start to turn. I backed away in quick judgement and as he turned around. His face pale and drained of life. The blood from his eyes was starting to burn the floors with every drop.

The smell of salt water and rotting flesh filled the room. The harbor started to shake as the storm was tearing through the town. The creature jumped over the bar revealing the keys to be on the wall behind him. As we wrestle the creature around the tavern, Tom grabs the keys. In one swift swing the creature sliced open Dale's stomach and started to devour his intestines. Maggie screams in horror as her husband lies lifeless on the tavern floor. Tom grabs her and drags her to the basement door, I shortly follow. The creature opened the door upstairs letting loose the demons upstairs in the brothel. Tom and I barely get the door shut as the hell spawn try to bust it down. The basement was dark and musty. The air was filled with the smells of an old graveyard and molded tombs. I was searching for a light as Tom fell over what seems to be a pile of debris. We move the cover to reveal a hidden chamber beneath the old wooden floors. The fog rushed through the hole and took over the room around us. What we soon discover would haunt any man's dreams for lifetimes to come. Millions of bodies, scattered around the moss-covered floor. The bodies belonged to all the legendary Captains that had their picture on the tavern's wall. Dismantled, crushed bones covered in maggots filled the floor around us. The water around us felt like cold steel brushing against the flesh. As we searched for a way out, a light at the end of the hall revealed a ladder back up to the boardwalk above. Maggie runs in a burst of excitement thinking it was the last of our troubles. Ole Tom screams for her to stop because she doesn't know what lies ahead.

As Maggie rushes quicker to the ladder, the water starts to tremble as something rises from the mist. It was Muriel, Ole Tom filled with joy tried to speak to her but with no response the air became crisp. Our bones chilled with what happened next. The creature revealed itself, with Muriel attached to its bulb. The sharp teeth peeked out of the darkness as the light exploded from Muriel's eye sockets and mouth. It catches Maggie by her foot, but Tom stabs it in the eye. I grabbed the musket and started to load it while I watched the creature sink its teeth right through Tom's body. Its black eyes peered into my soul, as I stood shaking in fear. Maggie distracts the beast as I finish loading the musket. With one final opportunity I strike, knowing that if I miss, I would have doomed us all. I scream to get its attention to give Maggie a chance to escape. As the creature runs for my quivering body, I shoot with one last rush of energy. I managed to hit it right in the eye, blinding it as I ran for the ladder. With my one chance of escaping becoming slim I started to climb. The beast grabbed my leg and started pulling me closer. Maggie reaches out her hands for me to latch on to, but I was too late. As I took my final stance, I turned the musket around and lunged at the beast with the bayonet. With the final blow to the creature the Tavern starts to collapse. Wood and pallets crashing around, our bodies as if the sky itself was falling. No chance of survival, I say my final goodbye to my dead crew and friends lying around me. The building is crashing as the screams from the creature haunt the waters. In my last shine of light there was a hand grabbing at my shirt. It takes a firm grip and pulls me out of the water. I was blinded by seaweed, dirt, and the salt from the unforgiving ocean. My vision was blurred for a few moments. As I started to regain my sight I saw Maggie at the end of the dock. Looking at me, with an everlasting look of joy on her face. The sky starts to crack as an unholy entity shaking the earth beneath its feet approaches from the storm. Unable to say a word, I fight to stand up. The beast draws closer and closer as I lose the motivation to move. Maggie turns around and starts to speak to me. As I investigate her tear-filled eyes, she seems to be relieved. I plead for her to move away from the edge of the harbor, and she tells me. "Not to worry, everything will be okay." In a state of utter shock and disbelief Maggie starts to turn. My body is frozen from the frightening scene of unnatural actions. As lightning fills the skies, it reveals the beasts' grotesque figure piece by piece. With one final glance I open my eyes to see Maggie in my face. In a shocked state I could not move, nor speak. She stares deep into my eyes. Revealing other worldly terrors, in the reflection of her lifeless eyes. She gets close to my ear and whispers in a faint tone.

"It's time to go Mr. Phillips. Your destiny awaits you."

Just like an ancient tomb, a loud bang shutters the environment around us making everything pitch black. I could feel the air leaving this world, and the ground becoming concrete. As I open my eyes I see a red light at the end of the path. As I get closer and closer to the light I hear fond memories, and cheers of my crew. As I get closer and closer to the light it seems to fade away. My memories seem to be dying with every step; the void is calling my name and it's the only noise left to hear. My sanity is slowly slipping away as I'm being torn apart by the empty feelings that surround me.

Am I in Heaven? Or is this my own personal Hell…

"Mr. Babbino"

The streets of New York always filled the night air with such noise. Noise that would hypnotize the mind and guide the bravest hearts to their wildest dreams. Love and excitement would hit the crisp winds as New Year's Eve dawned upon the city. Families and children preparing for the festivities that would bring in the new year. The shops were filled with bright lights, and a faint smell of ginger to caress the alleyways. Snow would gracefully cover the street signs and walkways. It almost seemed like angels came down from the Heavens and painted such a magnificent sight. As the city streets were filled with clutter, there was only one place no one would go. The Old Opera House near the end of town. The opera house was the city's main attraction for locals and travelers alike. There were beautiful performances that would leave the city in such a shock and awe. It was the grandest entertainment in New York, opening in 1925 and its final show was in 1958. Owned by the infamous Babbino family, which traveled to the country on a boat in the early 20s. They were all excellent performers, Vincent Babbino the father was the best piano player New York has ever laid its eyes upon. Bellavonte Babbino the mother had the voice of an angel; she would put on some of the best performances the world has ever seen.

Then there were the two children. Angelo Babbino and Jovanna Babbino were very odd children. They would never associate or play with the other kids in the neighborhood. Most of the time they stayed inside, making puppets and learning how to play music to hopefully one day join their parents on stage. It was December 30th, 1958, the Babbino family had to close the Opera house because they couldn't afford to keep it open. The business was slowly dying, and the town wanted them out so they could build new stores. Vincent had become old, and brittle. Sitting in his favorite chair just watching the snow fall upon the city like a comforting numbness to hide the sights that were once filled with so much life. One night after Vincent and Bellavonte finally tried to get some rest. Angelo was out working a late shift at the stockyard. He got off work at 1 am, expecting to go home and help his sister set up the decorations and get prepared for the festivities later in the day. As Angelo walks in the door, his sister is lying on the ground. Lifeless, the stab wounds were pouring blood onto the old oak floors like spilled paint spreading across an empty canvas. The smell of gasoline filled the room, constricting around his lungs and causing his vision to fade. He screams for help as he runs upstairs to check on his parents. He busts down the smoke covered door to see his father's throat torn apart, his mother in the corner gasping for air as what life she had left was seeping from her eyes. Angelo falls to his knees, accepting what is to come. With the drop of a pin, the building is engulfed in flames. The flames consumed the night sky as if heaven itself had caught fire. The next day during the fire Marshals investigation all 4 bodies were expected to be there on scene but had come up missing. They finally closed off the front doors and the building was left there to rot.

It's now 1962, Five years after the opera house fire that took the lives of the Babbino family. The city officials expected this year's New Year's celebration to be the biggest one this city has ever seen. After the business proposal for the new shops was turned down, they took all the extra money into their own pockets. The city air was filled with excitement and laughter over the anticipation for tonight's event. People from all over the country were expected to fill the city streets and join in on the bringing of the new year. Until the lights in the Opera House came on, after years of it just sitting there rotting away like any other common grave. The officials were in shock, telling the local authorities to investigate the area expecting it to be some local kids pulling a prank. As the police entered the front door it was dark, and dust filled the air in what seemed like an eternity of death. The ashes of the old furniture and family portraits covered the ground beneath them. Mold had covered the walls, and the smell of burnt flesh slithered its way into their nostrils. They walk upstairs to find a door, with gracious music coming from behind its golden glare. As they entered the room there was a beautiful dinner table set up in the middle of the room. The music was vibrating off the chandeliers and gracefully entering their ears.

As they continue to investigate, they see a man sitting at the Piano and a woman with an enchanting figure staring out the window. Her voice was something made by the gods themselves, almost in a complete trance the men sit at the table to admire their performance. As they start to eat the food that was prepared on the table, laughing and enjoying their glorious moment. The lights dim as a dark shadow presents itself in the room. The candles go out and the faint light haunts its surroundings like the winter dawn. The men look over at the window as the enchantress slowly turns her body towards them. Her face gets close to the light and the horrifying sights of this disfigured woman shatter their stance. The man on the piano had stopped playing but the music was still going, sending a chill down their spines. The vicious wind comes ripping through the room as a dark figure appears. It gets down and contorts its body and crawls towards them. The snapping of bones and gushing sound of rotting flesh was almost overpowering the music playing through the hall. Three of the men took out their guns and started shooting at the morbid creature crawling towards them. As the body falls, they start to feel a sign of relief, but coming from the bowels of the disfigured corpse was a sinister laugh. As they ran out the room a man with a burnt face appeared in front of them. Wearing an old orchestra suit and gloves covered in mold. The stench coming from his presence was overbearing, he ran full speed and started slicing the men one by one. Bullets and bright lights fill the room as the music devours the noise. Limbs and bones were being ripped apart as one man tried to escape. He barely makes it out the front door as a hand extends from the darkness and grabs the top of his head. As the fingers start to scale his face and the nails grip his flesh he is pulled back in. With his faint scream echoing through the streets like a gust of wind.

The night was still young; the city officials were getting ready for the annual party at the trinity hall. Not aware of the horrors that they sent the authorities into. They were all putting on their nice suits, imported shoes, even had watches with their names on it to show off their status. Their families were packing into the dining room as the New Years party was about to begin. Women and children were all laughing and dancing as the men were preparing for a toast. The waiters and hall staff were bringing in food carts as the glasses were entering the air. The smell of cheap wine and cigars filled the room and created a smog of delusions for fun and grandeur. As the clock struck down, the party went on. Everyone was sitting down, chewing down on their food as if it was the first meal they have ever seen. Children were throwing their food at each other as the adults were laughing and singing of their success.

The gold lights shined off their eyes, the moonlight filled their hearts with security. As the room started counting down from thirty, they started hearing strange noises from the ceiling, the sounds of angels stomping their feet. The windows blow open and the snow starts to cover its surroundings like moss in the open forest. The Hall staff seemed to disappear, and the children were hiding under the table not aware of the dangers that came next. The sounds from the ceiling got louder as the men and women looked up. They see a woman in a beautiful dress turning her head and spewing blood onto the table. Fingers and eyeballs were falling from her mouth onto the table below like the spring rain. Men and women were being slaughtered like lambs as music filled the room. Fire started piercing its way through the decorative walls. The townspeople cheered as they were counting down until the new year was drowning out the sounds of their agony. As the man in the orchestra suit busts through the front door he jumps on the dining room table. Skipping and kicking plates, singing along with the haunting music. He makes it to the end of the table and stares into the man's eyes. The man turned pale at the sight of him, the sweat pouring from his forehead hitting the ground like boulders off a cliff. He soon discovers whose eyes are staring into his soul. As the clock counts down to five. The mayor stutters:

"No, no this can't be real."

With the sharp blade piercing his rib cage he stares into his eyes.
The man in the suit says to him;

"Say it, say my name." With the mayor's final breath, he whispers.

"Angelo…"

As the clock strikes midnight and the city erupts with excitement for the new year. Fireworks are filling the night sky, children are dancing, the people are singing. He finally lays his head on the cold marble floor. The room starts to disappear, fading into a cold black abyss. All the bodies start to decay and the sound of celebration rings in his ears. He starts to remove the knife he placed in the mayor's rib cage and carves his family name into his chest. Smoke was filling the room and taking over every inch of the walls. As the flames rise from the depths of Hell that he once called home. His memory starts to fade as his childhood dreams become nightmares. Visions of his family welcoming him home with open arms, and a sense of nirvana courses through his body. The whole room is covered in flames, the flesh is starting to burn, and as the explosion begins; he kisses the mayor's forehead and utters the words.

"All'inferno con te Giuda"

"The Penthouse"

It was May 1988, Dana and David were excited to start their summer vacation after finishing their last semester of a grueling senior year of high school. Their final climb up the mountain before they are set loose into the real world. A world filled with adventure, opportunities and other ventures for these high school sweethearts to take part in. Dana was getting ready to go off to college to become a veterinarian while David had more timid, simple goals. He loved managing the local theater and working local town events throughout the holidays. David and Dana met their freshman year and have been inseparable since; it was love at first sight. A fire so pure and filled with determination, it almost seemed as if they both were invincible if they were together. They could take on the world. David and Dana were invited to a graduation party by their mutual friend Ellis. Ellis was always getting himself into trouble and finding new pranks to pull every year. He was very popular throughout high school and since his 18th birthday was the week before graduation, he wanted to have one last blowout before they all had to go their separate ways. Desperate to cling on to the "good times" he was going to pull out all the stops to have a party that no one at school would ever forget. A party so flamboyant, and bizarre that it would be told in the halls of that school for years to come.

David was busy working his usual late shift at the theater, enjoying some popcorn as he snuck off to attend a showing of "Killer Klowns from Outer Space". Business was kind of slow on Sundays, so he always enjoyed grabbing a few snacks and kicking back with the newest releases while his boss Jerry was away. As David goes to take a drink, he feels a hand on his shoulder and is shocked to see Ellis there. But Ellis wasn't alone, Ellis was joined by a few friends from school and David's girlfriend Dana. They all sit around David to share the details of the big party with him. David saw this as the perfect event to propose to Dana, since it would probably be the last time that they would all be together with their friends before they move away and start their lives.
Ellis shares a story with the group. About a killer location he knows of on the outskirts of town. The Penthouse, apparently it was an old VHS rental store that was shut down in 1982. Ellis proceeds to share its extravagant backstory, filled with big laughs and warm feelings of the cozy neon lights reflecting off the glass. Ellis' dad used to go take him there when he was little. Every payday he would go there with his father, and they would rent the scariest movies they could find. Grab a handful of candy and other delicious snacks. Ellis felt tremendous joy as he excitedly sat back reminiscing about the smell of freshly cooked popcorn with large amounts of butter. The weirdly tacky carpet, covered

with a rainbow of colors and how they would reflect off the blacklights. The sounds of the arcade machines drowning out whatever movie was playing on the TVs around the shop. Everyone could sense the aroma with every detail that he shared. He proceeds to tell them about one of his favorite things in the old rental store. A giant, animatronic Flamingo with a sign above its head that read its name "Paulie the Mingo " sat in the back of the store. If you put in a quarter, it would belt out one liner like "Be kind, Rewind" or "Don't be late, return the tape by its date!" and it always had a bowl of candy beside it. You were allowed to take one treat per visit, any more than that and you had to hand the cashier an extra twenty-five cents. Paulie was on all the merchandise for the store. T shirts, stickers, posters, you name it! As Ellis proceeds to tell him about how wonderful this store was, it suddenly starts taking a dark turn. Ellis tells the group that there were rumors on why the store closed. Stories of the mob being involved, the cashier was attacked by a customer, and other wild bits.

Years later the truth would come out, the owner of the VHS store had suffered from a range of mental illnesses. His wife went missing, which resulted in him taking his own life by hanging himself in his office at the store. The cashier found him the next morning when he went to clock in and start his shift. The store closed a week later, with no family to keep it up and running. It has become a shell of the past; a place filled with memories but simply left to collect dust from years of neglect. Since then, local kids have always shared stories of ghost sightings and other paranormal experiences when driving by the store late at night. Rumors of hearing the arcade machines turned on, the neon lights flickering, and some say they can see the manager standing in the doorway at night. Waiting there for eternity until the love of his life finally returns to him.

David, Dana and the other kids from school laugh and scoff as Ellis shares this story. One of the kids says "Yeah right" as the other bellows laughter out loud enough to echo in the halls of the theater. Dana replies with, 'Yeah, what is this? A scary story for kids? We all know none of this is real Ellis." Ellis then turns to drop the big news on them, that The Penthouse will be the location for his big Graduation/Birthday party. All of them look at each other perplexed by this news, wondering if Ellis is serious or if this is another one of his jokes? They all nervously agree on the idea, trying to play off that some of them are uncomfortable with this idea after the stories Ellis has shared. Ellis jumps up in excitement and says, "See you at the party!" as he takes David's drink and happily dances his way out the door. David takes a moment and waits for everyone to leave. Thinking that right now might be a good time to propose to Dana, in an empty theater with a movie playing in the background. The same theater where they shared their first date, their first kiss, the location has such a sentimental value behind it.As David works up the gumption to execute on his plans, Dana gets a sense of his next move and awkwardly jumps up. "Hey David, your shift is almost over, I think it's time that you closed up. Wanna walk me home?" David, with a bit of disappointment in his tone, agrees and continues to close the theater. David and Dana take their usual walk home in the crisp night air, with a bit of a chill flowing down the street from the nearby lake. They share their thoughts about the party; Dana seems excited about the event. As the conversation continues David brings up an idea on what happens after the party. It is their final summer break; David asks Dana how she feels about college and more. Dana shares with David how excited she is to go and become a veterinarian. She goes on to mention how she can't wait to move which takes David for a spin because she has never mentioned this before. David always assumed that she would be attending college locally so he could continue managing the theater. Hoping one day to take over as the head whenever Jerry decides to retire.

Dana tells David that she didn't want to be "stuck in the past" that her life could be so much different somewhere else. She was going to college, she was attending plays, concerts and more to find herself in these settings. She told David that maybe things outside of that small town would be so much better for her. It was time for her to let go of everything there, and move on from the cage she felt like she was in. David was heartbroken by the statement because her letting go of everything meant she would be letting go of him as well. David tucks the engagement ring back into his pocket, thinking that maybe this wasn't the best idea now. Maybe he could try later, who knows how things were going. Everyone is so focused on graduating, college, traveling, bigger lives and careers. The next few months of their lives would be so unpredictable. So, he thought that for now it would be safer to not mention it at all.

They slowly approach Dana's gate; the same gate he has walked her to a million times in the past 4 years. They exchange a hug but when David goes in for their usual goodnight kiss Dana backs away. In the awkward silence Dana says goodnight to David, and that she would call him tomorrow to see what time he would pick her up for the party. David turns and walks home, with such a feeling of dread and despair in his heart. He had no idea what to do next, he planned out his whole life with this girl. She was the love of his life, but now everything he thought he knew about her suddenly changed. On the drop of a dime, his whole world was flipped upside down. David gets home and turns the key to his front door. His best friend, Tabitha, who was a beautiful grey tabby cat, was sure to meet him upon his entrance. Going back and forth between his legs, showing her excitement for his arrival. He gives her a few pats and a treat then goes to bed. With a lot on his mind he pops in his cassette of The Cure's latest album "Kiss me, Kiss me, Kiss me." He lets the haunting melodies of Robert Smith's voice sing him to sleep for another night like he has many times before. The next morning David wakes up to a knock at his door. His parents are nowhere to be seen; the halls feel so empty and cold with no one to greet him or give him a "Goodmorning". He goes to the door after the knocks continue, as he opens the door there is no one there. David, confused at what just happened, looks down to see

Tabitha picking at a package on the porch. The package reads, "Watch Me" in an old bag from The Penthouse. David assumes that this must be from Ellis, so he takes the tape out and pops it in his VHS player. The tape takes a minute to start, static from the TV fills the halls as he sees the silhouette of a man on his TV screen. Someone moving through the static with a low tone voice in the background. As he attempts to turn the tape off it finally starts to play. It shows the countertop to an old beat-up shelf. Bright pink and blue neon lights light up the room and then Ellis pops up from behind the desk.

"Surprise!" he screams, as he tries to get off a cheap jump scare.

As the tape continues, Ellis shares the opening to his invitation.

"Hello! If you have received this tape, then YOU have been invited to the final party of our Senior Year down at The Penthouse!"

David stares in disbelief as he ponders to himself on why Ellis would go this far to make a tape for his party. Especially for everyone attending. As the tape rolls on, the audio gets distorted as Ellis shares the address to the location. David proceeds to ignore the tape and continues to enjoy his breakfast that he was making while watching it. He almost burnt his toast because he was so distracted by the tape Ellis made. A loud noise and scratch come from the TV, a deep tone voice says "PAY ATTENTION" as David is looking away while eating his meal. In utter shock David looks around to see no one there. He looks at the screen and it nears its end with Ellis sharing that the Penthouse is located on "1952 Broadway St." Ellis ends his little video with a classic line he mentioned yesterday. "Please be kind, rewind" and "Don't be late, return the tape by its date!" The date on the tape was marked for today. May 28th, 1988.

David gets up from the table and cleans up from breakfast. He puts food in Tabitha's bowl and grabs his car keys. He is scrambling around for his favorite pair of sneakers as he gets a call from Dana. "Hello?" David says shakingly. "Hey Babe!" Dana greets David with such enthusiasm as if she didn't say anything off the night before. David and Dana continues to talk about their plans for tonight, and what they will wear. David asks Dana if she also received a tape. Dana is so confused by David's question, "What tape?" "What are you talking about?" David tells Dana about the tape he received this morning, he tells her it might be from Ellis, but she brushes it off. Assuming that David is just making this whole thing up, to make Ellis seem weird or crazy. David says that she should come over so he can show her the tape, to prove to her that he isn't making it up. Dana shows up thirty to forty minutes later eager to see the infamous tape David was mentioning during their call. David sits down with Dana and proceeds to tell her about the package he received earlier that morning. All the things he saw and heard, and about the fact that Ellis was on the tape. He goes to show her the tape, but it isn't working. Dana smirks and says,

"Did you not rewind it?" David gets up and laughs, "Yeah, how silly of me. Sorry." David proceeds to rewind the tape, static blasts through the TV. Distorted noises, sounds like machines crashing together and glass breaking off the floor. Once the tape is finished rewinding, he hits play and nothing happens. There is no video, no noise, nothing. He takes the tape out to see what's wrong with it. As he opens the back of the VHS, he sees that there is no film at all, he checks the VCR assuming that it might have been stuck in there and he finds nothing at all. Dana expressing her agitation asks "Can we please go get lunch, I'm starving. I don't care about the stupid tape." David in complete disbelief puts the tape back in the bag and throws it in the back of his car.

It's now nighttime. David and Dana are on their way to the party listening to some of David's tapes. David figures since they have a little bit of time, he should talk to her about the things she said the night before. David waits a few minutes to conjure up the courage to speak about what's on his mind and Dana turns up the music. David says "Hey..." as time goes on, he tries again. 'Hey, can we talk about last night?" After Dana finally hears him, she asks him what he wants to talk about. David is wondering what she meant by "Leaving everything behind" and "Letting go". Dana tells David that she was too afraid to have this talk, but she thinks now is a good time. Dana tells David that she has tried to make this relationship work but she wants to take a break. She tells David that she needs time to find herself, to go out there and discover things. See how different her life could be. She was sure to remind David that it has nothing to do with him. In her eyes, he was perfect. But, feelings change, that doesn't mean she didn't love him, things are just different now. David has no idea how to respond; he sits in silence as they continue their drive. David utters that "True love, it never changes" Dana asks him if they can just go to the party and have a good time that night, to not think about anything else. David nods and continues

They both arrive at the parking lot. The Penthouse lights up the dark streets with its bright neon lights. The smell of popcorn and cigarettes filled the air as a bunch of the kids from school were hanging out in the front of the building. There wasn't another store or house for miles, David was shocked to see how well Ellis cleaned up the place as they proceeded to walk in. Music is blaring, as people are playing arcade games and slamming on the pinball machines. Popcorn and other snacks cover the bright carpet on the floor. Everyone is drinking punch from the table and having a good time with Ellis nowhere in sight. David goes to walk with Dana, but her friends come up and interrupt with a conversation. David continues to get a drink from the punch bowl. It's filled with this bright purple soda; it has a fantastic mixture of grape flavoring with a hint of Cinnamon. David couldn't recall ever having something like this before. As time goes on, there is a voice over the intercom telling everyone to proceed to the back. As they all entered the room, there was a stage and tables from where the store would host events, birthday parties and more. The lights dimmer down as a small eruption of applause takes over the room and Ellis hits the stage.

"Welcome to The Penthouse ladies, gentlemen, and other oddities in attendance! Let's have one last night together, one last hurrah, one last rager!" Ellis proceeds to shoot confetti all over the room as the music deafens out the surrounding noise of the crowd. Everyone starts dancing, jumping up and down. David's vision starts to fade as the purple lights take over his sight. The room becomes distorted; people's faces are melting. Their hands are rotting; eye sockets filled with insects. David starts to fade in and out of conscientiousness, he turns to look at Dana and her tongue falls out of her mouth as it turns into a bunch of maggots. David passes out and hits the floor. As he opens his eyes, the room is flooded with screams of terror. There are loud thuds as bodies are hitting the floor, David is trying to regain his sight amid all the chaos. When he awakes, he sees someone swinging an axe, someone in the Paulie Mingo Mascot outfit is killing everyone in sight. His eyes are pure red as blood and other sludge drips from his teeth. The pale pink feathers are now covered in their friend's blood, as this monster stands over the pile of bodies it is leaving behind.

David gets up to run as the axe wielding maniac picks someone up by their throat and slams their face through the arcade machine. David, still with distorted vision, sees Dana hiding in the corner and they run into the back storage room. David is covering the door as Dana is freaking out. She is screaming "Get the bugs! Get them off me! Please, they are in my eyes!" They are eating my tongue!" David tries to calm her down and keep her quiet, so the person outside doesn't hear them. David convinces Dana to follow him through the storage room, their minds still altered; they are lost in a labyrinth and don't know the way out. The music is still blaring in the main rooms; the bass is drowning out the sounds of everyone else's screams. Dana and David make their way into an office area. Trying to find any way out but all the windows and doors are boarded up. They hear a noise at the door they just came through, Dana goes to see if it's one of their friends. As David screams "NO!" an axe gets shoved through the front of the locked door. Dana screams as David grabs her hand and they run towards the back room.

David knocks a bunch of stuff over to hopefully delay the killer. They hide in an old, dark room. It has a faint smell of mold, rust and a strong smell of rot. There is a liquid on the floor that neither of them can see. They both look for some sort of light source in the room. Dana finds the light switch and as the light fills the room, they see such a visceral inducing scene. There is an old, rotting body hanging from the ceiling. Entrails drip to the floor as flies go in and out of its mouth. The neck was barely staying on the noose; it was stuck too, as the body was slowly detaching itself. It was the manager from the stories. They look on his desk for some sort of keys and they see a picture of the manager with his Family. A wife and son, happily on a vacation to the Grand Canyon dated June 6th, 1979. As David and Dana search deeper into the desk they hear banging on the door. The killer approaches as he swings the axe through the wooden door. David and Dana are cornered with nowhere to go, they find a basement vent behind them hidden in the murky water.

David rushes Dana through the vent as the killer busts through the door. They both fall for what seems like ages before they hit the ground. They end up in a slightly dimmed room, surrounded by toys, games, TVs, and other collectibles. Posters on the wall, soda cans everywhere with moldy pizza. The smell of body odor and sewage fills the room as they search for an exit. David finds a flashlight in a cabinet on the far-left side of the room. Hoping to find an exit even quicker now they rush to the other side. David falls, and the flashlight rolls to the right-hand side of the room. He grabs the light and as he looks up, he sees a shrine on his wall. Hundreds of pictures of The Manager and his family. But the wife's face is cut out of every single picture and replaced with pictures of... Dana? David is shaken to his core as he continues to see this wild shrine dedicated to his partner, he then finds an old newspaper dated March 1st, 1982. "Local video shop owner commits suicide after Wifes disappearance." "The ongoing investigation on the whereabouts of Mrs. Verone continues after the passing of her late husband" David continues to search through all the pictures and newspaper articles on the wall trying to piece it all together.

Dana sees the wall and is absolutely disgusted by the shrine. The thought of this person being so obsessed with her was repulsive and utterly unbearable. David grabs her hand and encourages her to continue with him to find an exit. They find a crawl space that leads to a passage under the street. As they continue the only company they have now are the sewer rats and awful smells from the musty water below. They are making their way through this maze of filth as they stumble across a box. David, being curious of what could be in there, proceeds to try and open it. As he pulls back the rotting wood, a strange liquid pours all over him. It's a skull, with a wedding ring and a small note. The note reads, "For the love of my life, may we be together forever. In this life and the next. Love, Paul Verone" The video store manager's wife wasn't missing at all. He murdered her and hid her body beneath his store. Then killed himself to be with her forever. David tries to bring the head with them as they find a ladder out of this hell hole. As they proceed to climb, they end up in the storage house behind the video store. The back door is padlocked shut, so they must make their way to the front of the building, hopefully avoiding the killer at all costs. David assumes that the body in the office might not be the managers at all. Maybe he is the one killing people, how else would there be another body hanging in the office all these years later? David grabs Dana by the hand and they make it back to the stage room. He covers their eyes as they step over the bodies of all their friends. There are bones, guts, and limbs everywhere with broken glass. The room that was once filled with the pleasant smells of popcorn and candy now smells like a morgue. They quietly make it back to the front of the store and see that they have a clear exit. As they proceed to the front door, Dana stops and pukes all over the floor. That strange purple liquid from earlier is all over the place. She starts to shake, foam flying from her mouth. David is quick to grab her and carry her to the front. As they get close to the door, an axe barely misses the front of his face. David drops to the floor while dropping Dana to the other side. The killer swings the axe towards David as the pale pink blood covered feathers fly in the air. David dodges the swings and jumps over the counter. As the killer goes to the other side, David with a brave attempt throws the cash register at the killer's head. Dana gets up to the door and opens it. "DAVID LET'S GO, HURRY!"

They both run out the front door for their escape. They both run to David's car, David goes to unlock the door but can't find his keys. They are miles away from town, there is no way they could outrun the killer on foot. David breaks out the car window, as a last attempt he tries to hotwire his car. He starts it, and Dana jumps in. As they go to speed off, an axe gets slammed through the passenger side window and chops Dana's head in half. David spins out, knocking the killer back but crashing his car into the tree across the street. David looks up at the gruesome sight of his lover's face split in half. Right above the lip, separating the nose and mouth. Her jaw hangs low, blood drips from her mouth and her right eyeball pops out on the dashboard. David crawls out of the car as the front of it catches fire. He crawls down the street away from the car in front of the store. He hears a loud roar behind him.

"LOOK AT WHAT YOU MADE ME DO"

The killer bellows from the pit of their stomach. David turns around facing the killer, they finally take off their mask to reveal their identity. To his shock, the killers Identity was revealed to be his friend Ellis. David is laying on the ground speechless, blood flying out of his mouth with every cough. Ellis screams,

"YOU KNOW I WATCHED HIM DO IT TOO? I WATCHED HIM
KILL MY MOM!"

David, still confused and barely able to move, continues

"He was so angry that my dad took her from him. That he had to take her away from all of us! He was right, my dad did deserve it and so didn't she. She was nothing but a liar!"

"HE WAS THE BEST UNCLE IN THE WORLD"
"DANA SHOULD'VE BEEN WITH ME, ME, NOT YOU!"
"YOU MADE ME KILL HER; THIS IS YOUR FAULT!"

Ellis picks up the axe and walks towards David.

"I'M GOING TO MAKE YOU PAY!"

Ellis lifts the axe above his head before he is stopped. He turns around and laughs as heavy footsteps approach him. He starts laughing maniacally as the footsteps draw near. "Are you proud of me?" "Look at my progress!" He screams with Joy. "I did it!" The footsteps stop as a giant shadow engulfs over Ellis. Ellis backs up and cowers, he proceeds to ask. "What is it? What did I do wrong?" David still can't figure out who is standing in front of Ellis. All he can hear is Ellis' voice as the fire roars behind him. Ellis starts to scream.

"NO! NO! I DID EVERYTHING RIGHT; I DID EVERYTHING YOU WANTED!"

His scream infects David's ear as they echo through the abandoned streets. Ellis' head and spine are ripped completely out of his body as a terrifying screech is released from the figure in front of him. David passes out as the tall figure walks in front of him. Sensing that this is his end, he welcomes the heat from the flames behind him and prepares for the worst as he passes out. David wakes up the next day in the hospital. Lost and confused on how he got there. He tries to scramble out of bed but can barely move. His body feels like it was filled with cement, his parents rush to his side filled with Joy that their baby boy was still alive. David asks what happened as the Chief of Police walks in. He starts to question David on what happened last night, and David explains that his friend Ellis started killing everyone, but his memory is foggy. The officer confirms that they found the shrine and all the bodies. David asks where Ellis is, the police chief goes outside for a minute to talk to his other officers. David's parents cradle him, so glad that their son somehow survived these horrible events. The police Chief walks back in and says that unfortunately it's almost impossible to identify all the bodies considering how much damage was done. That the only thing they could identify was a head that they found inside the store.

The police Chief shared with them as they arrived on scene, they walked inside the store and towards the back wall they found Ellis's head. The animatronic Paulie Mingo was holding it in his treat bowl. The family is mortified as the officers continue to ask "David who could've done that if Ellis was the killer?" They also found the murder weapon still in his car and drugs in his system. Along with everyone else who was at the party. They place David under arrest for the murders of 25 students, including the murder of Mrs. Verone. David screams and shouts that he is innocent, that Ellis was the murderer, that they had to believe him! As the Chief goes to exit the room, he recommends that the family contact a good lawyer and that they would be back to get him once he recovers from his injuries. David has lost all sense on what happened, he mutters to himself... "Did I kill them? No, Ellis did, I'm sure of it." as he tries to recall his memory, the entire night is nothing but a blur to him. It all seemed like some sick and twisted game someone was playing on him.

He couldn't have killed all those people. David screams out in his bed "WHY CAN'T I REMEMBER!" "I DIDN'T KILL THEM I SWEAR" he starts to panic and then a nurse walks in. She says to David, "This package just arrived for you." David questions as to who could have sent it. She replies. "I have no idea sweetie; we just found it in the mail deposit box with your name on it." David rushes and tears open the package. A fixed chill enters the room as there is a tingle down his spine. It's a tape, and it has a message written on it. "Be kind, Rewind." "Don't be late, return it by the date!" with "October 19th, 1988" on the back. David has a nervous breakdown and screams at the top of his lungs, "NO, NO NOT AGAIN!" David runs full speed at the window, attempting to take his own life but the hospital staff and police restrain him back into his bed. It is now October, 5 months after the murders. David hasn't spoken a word since that day in the hospital.

Today is his trial, October 19th, 1988. The judge receives new evidence to show the court. A tape, found in The Penthouse lobby. When the judge shows the tape to the court, you see the Killer slaughtering everyone at the party. Slamming someone's head through an arcade machine, cutting another one's leg off. The scene is horrible. At the end of the video, you see Dana running for the exit of the store, with the killer not too far behind. The killer removes their mask, and it is revealed to be David. David screams out in court "NO, NO I DIDN'T KILL HER, I LOVED HER! ELLIS DID IT! ELLIS DID!" The judge has David removed from the court as the families of the victims all scream and throw things at him after what they just witnessed on the tape. David is sentenced to 100 years in Prison for the murders he committed. With no chance of parole. It is now March 27th, 2013. It has been 25 years since the murders; David is now 43 years old and unable to speak. For the first time ever, someone has sent him a package today, he goes into his cell after collecting his gift and opens it. It's a VHS Tape... with "Be Kind, Rewind" written on the front with the date 10/19/18 written on the back. Next to the VHS tape was a bobblehead of the mascot Paulie Mingo. Later that night David proceeds to take his own life in his cell.

Forever trying to prove his own innocence, or his insanity...

"Case #1: The Manor"

It was a brisk, rained filled fall morning, November 10th, 1957. Randy and Michael are at their favorite local diner to get their usual breakfast. The biscuit and gravy combo with a large black coffee, they have been ordering the same thing ever since they started working on the force together 10 years ago. In the middle of their breakfast, they get a call about a body that was discovered at an abandoned Manor. Randy and Michael pick up their coffees and rush out the front door because crimes like these didn't happen too often in their small town. Randy starts the car as Michael grabs his radio, the duo is packed and ready to go for whatever events lie ahead of them. The old Manor was something both men grew up hearing about. Countless tales, rumors, and scary stories that kept them up at night. They both figured all of that was simply a way for kids to stay away from the property or, a fun way to tease your friends late at night at the slumber party. As they pull up to their first exit, the radio in the car suddenly cuts out. A loud flash of light and total silence takes over the area, both men are frantic as they look around wondering what just happened. As Randy goes to radio into the station the car radio screeches out with loud static, and Michael covers his ears. They both take a minute to step out of the car and get a breath of fresh air. Especially after Randy's excessive smoking on their journey there.

The street ahead was hard to see, there was a heavy fog from the early morning rain. They were accustomed to sights like these growing up in Washington. There were no cars coming from either direction, no noises to be heard. They were left with nothing more than the moisture in the air and the smell of the water from the river nearby. They both figured that maybe there was some radio interference from the towers in the mountains, or the possibility that maybe they are too far away from the town. Either way, the men got back in their vehicle and continued to their investigation. They pull up to a dirt road, the same dirt road they heard about in the infamous stories from when they were children. The road leading to the manor was riddled with muddy tracks, stray rocks, and haunted by tales told by all the city folk over the years. As they trekked up the hill it felt like they were in that car for centuries, they finally pulled into the front of the Manor with the metal gate closed and there was no one to be seen. Randy picks up his Radio and tries to call the officer that was on the scene but there was no response. Michael has the brilliant idea that he could simply climb up the vine covered walls beside the gate and open it from the other side. Randy warns him of potential injury considering the condition of the wall itself. The stonework seems like it has stood the test of time, with all its cuts and dirt patches going down the trim with moldy vines stuck to it to almost form some sort of seal or cover.

Michael continues with his plans and climbs the wall, shortly after he meets Randy at the front gate and lets him in. The two carry on to the front of the house and have yet to find anyone on the scene. Randy goes up to the front door and grabs onto its handle. For some reason the metal handle is so cold, it burns his hand the minute he pulls the handle. Miachel laughs it off as a simple after effect from the wild weather they have been having, and they proceed into the main hall. The manor is so dark and covered in dust. With pale maroon walls and silver lining festering through every crack in its surface. The hardwood floors creak and crumble with every step, echoing through the halls of the manor as if they had a story to tell. A haunting melody comes from the living room as Randy and Michael continue to search around for any sign of life. Randy and Michael go into the living room to investigate the noise, and they find a singular rocking chair, in the corner of the room facing the fireplace. The fireplace was riddled with coal dust and cobwebs that covered a good bit of the wall as well. Randy walks up to the chair and sits in it. He can feel the cold wood pressing down on his suit as he goes to pull out a cigarette. He struggles to light it due to a breeze coming from inside the manor. Michael holds his hands over the lighter to assist Randy in his efforts, the two laugh as nothing they do seems to work now. Randy decides it's time to move on and see if they can find out where the sound was coming from. As they proceed through the rooms of the manor, each one is filled with some sort of history from the families that used to roam these halls. Pictures, letters, clothes, toys, fancy imported furniture, all ruined by years of abandonment and neglect.

Randy eventually takes a wrong turn down the left wing and loses sight of Michael, he yells out to see if his partner can hear him with no avail. Randy sprints down the hallway to see if Michael was still in the master bedroom but Michael was gone. Randy yells out once more to see if he can get any sort of response and his efforts were futile because if Michael went to the other side of the manor there would be no way for his calls to be heard. Randy slowly loses his patience thinking that Michael is pulling another one of his jokes again and decides to return to the main hall. As he walks down the corridor he hears faint whispers in the corners of the halls, quick to turn around and catch Michael he turns to see nothing. There is no one there at all. Rage filled and confused he continues down the path and ends up going in a loop, he ends up in the same exact corridor no matter which direction he ran in.

Randy is slowly starting to lose his cool over the situation and goes to sit on the bed. As he sits on the bed, dust and smoke fill the room as he struggles to breathe. His vision gets blurry and suddenly the world is dark. His heart is pounding out of his chest, echoing like war drums on the frontlines. He is taken over by a chill and falls to the floor, curled up into the fetal position. He is doing everything he can to slow down his breathing. As he catches his breath, he feels a warm touch on his shoulder and a whisper in his ear. The voice shatters his ear drums as he is shoved into the hole in the ground. The fall seems like it goes on for ages as the room spins. The environment is slowly taken over by a musty black slime that fills in all the holes and cracks. Sounds of water crashing all around him as a visceral twist bends his reality into shape. He can hear people talking, laughing, screaming as he plummets deeper into the abyss. His body crashes into the earth as if he was a meteor breaking their earth's atmosphere. A hole opens in his chest and strange tentacle-like appendages come from the black walls and grab each one of his ribs one by one. They suddenly pull their grip back and hoist Randy in the air like a piece of art on display at a museum. A loud vibration comes from the pit in front of him as his eyes and ears start to bleed. His heart exposed, literally beating out of his chest as the tentacles pulled his ribs tighter. A figure emerges from the pit; there is a heavy sound of something wet and slimy crawling around the floors. As the figure pulls closer to Randy's face, he sees that it is Michael. Utterly shocked and unable to speak, Randy looks at Michael as if he is a beast from a story. An unfathomable abomination that could never have been crafted by the hands of God.

As Michael gets closer an overbearing feeling of dread fills the room. Michael grabs Randy by the face and whispers to him in such an unholy tone. "There is something rotting inside you." Randy tries to scream but no noise comes out, the vibration in the room is deafening as Michael grabs Randy by the throat and ascends to the ceiling. Michael throws Randy against the fireplace and crashes through the doorway. Bright lights shutter through the room as if someone was taking pictures of these events. Randy's bones were snapping, and his skin was burning as if every touch from the tentacles was filled with acid. Michael screams out in pain and proclaims, "It has to be taken out!" as he falls to the ground. Randy uses every bit of his strength to run to the front door, but Michael catches him in the corner of his eyes. Michael grabs Randy by the ankles and pulls him back in. He's scratching and clawing at his own eyes as his teeth fall out of his head. His body turns thin and yellow as his cheeks and hair thin out, he screams as he bashes his dilapidated hands on the ground.

Randy stares in horror as Michaels body falls apart, twisting, turning, and breaking with every move. Tentacles seeping from different parts of his body, his eyes melting away. As Michael turns to Randy, he slams him into the wall. Black powder was released from the old wooden boards and a strange symbol appeared on Michael's chest. Randy, unable to move, must bear witness to this strange transformation. His partner on the force for over 10 years turned into some sort of creature. The house starts to crumble as the walls cave in, Michaels new, deformed body slams through its surroundings. He screams out...

"THERE IS SOMETHING ROTTING!" "TAKE IT OUT!"

Confused by his friend's words, Randy finally gets the strength to get up. He grabs a broken board from the wall and runs at Michael. Michael knocks him back as the ceiling above him collapses. Randy goes to the other side and sees a hole in Michael's stomach revealing an organ lined in a dark purple coating. Thinking back to Michael's words Randy plunges forward and stabs the organ with the broken board. He didn't have time to have second thoughts or feel any remorse. This... thing wasn't Michael anymore. As the creature bellows out a cry all the glass in the house shatters, the earth beneath their feet starts to crumble as this strange purple substance fills the room. The creature lets out a violent roar as it explodes into ash, knocking Randy out of the bay windows and into the front yard of The Manor. The building has collapsed like a war-torn base, rubble and glass flying everywhere. Faint screams and other disgusting sounds filled the area. As things suddenly go quiet, Randy lies motionless in the yard. Staring up to the Heavens as Snow begins to fall on him.

Randy faints from the events but is suddenly woken up with a jolt! "The manor is still there?" He asks himself. He wakes himself up as if he had a bad dream or was hallucinating on some sort of drugs. He stands up and goes towards the front door, once he steps outside it is snowing. He is finally able to light up his cigarette and goes to his car. Michael is there waiting for him with his coffee from the diner they visited earlier. Michael informs Randy that he had an asthma attack while he was upstairs and passed out. Michael claims he carried Randy downstairs and laid him on the couch and called for an ambulance to come check on him, but it would be a while due to the snow. Randy brushes this off and tells Michael about the wild dream he just had. He says "It must have been a dream, right? There ain't no way any of that was real." Michael and him both laugh as they get in the car. Randy starts up the engine and waits for it to get warm as he grabs for another cigarette. He turns on the Radio hoping to hear some pleasant tunes after his traumatic experience, but the noise is fuzzy. He can hear a faint song coming from beneath the static as he twists the knobs to find a better signal. The only lyrics he can make out are from the song "Walkin After Midnight" by Patsy Cline. The radio static gets louder and louder as Michael gets in the car. Randy starts to pull off. They make it down the dirt road and are about to reach their exit as the radio echoes in his ears, repeating the same lyric. Mimicking an alarm clock going off in the morning, it was ringing in his ears. Michael sings out in an unbearable tone as the car spins out of control. Randy's line of sight is diminished by the snowstorm; he can't hear anything over the roar of the radio. Michael is laughing in his seat as they twist and turn down the hill. The car tips over the hillside and crashes into the bank below. Randy wakes up a short time later with the car upside down, his suit soaked from the murky river. He goes to the passenger side of the car and looks for Michael, but he isn't there. Randy climbs up the hill to get back on the main road, with the snow blurring his vision he marches forward to their exit. As Randy finally walks across the line from the exit, all the snow is gone. It suddenly started raining, water was crashing all around him as he frantically looked around in a state of confusion. He was suddenly back in front of the diner with his keys in his hand ready to get into his car. Watching Michael exit the diner as he grabbed their coffees, Randy breaks out in a cold sweat as he feels a cold breeze rush through his body. Randy looks down, and his heart is gone. There is nothing there, but a void made of decomposing flesh. The hole is engulfed by black mold, and he feels something moving inside. He reaches in to pull out whatever is lurking inside of his chest, and as he reaches further in, he can feel the flesh on his arm being burned away. He reaches deeper and deeper, his lungs fill with smoke and his face turns red, then purple. Randy collapses to the ground and Michael rushes to his aid. A few people from the diner rush out to assist them, Michael starts performing CPR. Michael does the best that he can until the ambulance arrives, once the paramedics show up, they rush him to the hospital. Randy died on the way to the hospital due to a heart attack.

Michael gets the news from the doctor and takes it upon himself to contact Randy's family. It was only right considering how long they have been friends. Michael pulls up to the front door and knocks three times. Randy's wife Debby answers the door and is surprised to see him. As she looks around, she notices that Randy isn't with him and asks if he is still at the office. Michael proceeds to ask if he may walk in. Debby welcomes him like she has a hundred times before, but makes her kids go to their room. Michael sits down with her to inform her of her husband's passing. She cries out hysterically unable to accept the news she received, as Michael grabs her to stop her from hitting the floor, he holds her next to the kitchen countertop. She cries into Michaels arms and proceeds to hug him. Michael can feel her warm but heartbroken tears run down his arm. She suddenly becomes quiet and stops crying, Michael asks Debby if she is okay, then assumes she is in shock. Debby leans up to Michael's ear and lets off a cold breath that sends a chill down his spine and whispers.

"*There is something rotting in you*."

Then inserts the knife into his abdomen, she twists the knife deeper as Michaels body crumbles to the floor. She stands over him with the knife in hand, Michael starts to lose what consciousness he has left. He stumbles upon his words as he asks Debby, "Why?" Debby looks down at him and replies.

"It has to be taken out."

"The Root Cellar"

Jonthan was only ten years old when he had to move into his grandparents' family home. Jonathan and his mother were forced to move out of their house because the bills were becoming too much of a burden. A single mother trying to work a part time job while paying for a big house in the woods made the task almost impossible. Jonathan wasn't too thrilled about the big life changes he was about to face. He moved around a lot as a kid but, there was only one place that he can recall where he truly felt at home. From the age of five until he was eight Jonathan and his family lived in a yellow house on the hill right across the street from his grandparents. He had a lot of fond memories there over the years. One memory he always kept close to his heart were the ones that took place in the summer. In his memory it would be the middle of June, he would wake up on a nice, breezy summer morning. Jonathan would mosey out of his warm and toasty bed then hop in the shower. Once he was done, he would put on some shorts and a sweater his sister gave him that had a basketball logo on it.

Jonathan didn't watch basketball too much back then, but he loved the design on the sweater and would wear it quite often. Once he finished his morning routine he would pull out his foldable lawn chair that he used to play video games and sit right in front of the TV. His mom would make eggs and bacon for breakfast as he watched his favorite Saturday morning cartoons. The smells of summer would fill the air as the breeze would sweep beneath the window seal and gracefully make its presence known throughout the room. After he consumed his breakfast Jonathan would turn on his game system while his mom played solitaire on the family computer that his sister won from a competition at school. Later in the day he would play outside with his cousins and bask in that warm summer sun before settling down for the night and having dinner while the sun sets. These toasty summer afternoons are something he thinks about quite often. There was that feeling in the air, the taste, the smells, the entire thing was unforgettable. Jonathan didn't know how to really feel about the idea of the afterlife, but in his mind, he could choose what his own personal heaven would be. It would be those summer afternoons in that bright yellow house. He would stay there for all eternity if he could.

Then came that dreadful day that he had to move. They were so close to finally getting the house, it was right at their fingertips until one day they received a call, and the owner explained to them that they had to leave because he was in the middle of a divorce and his wife got the house. Jonathan was absolutely devastated by this news. They eventually found a house in the woods two blocks away but that was only a temporary solution as well.

When the day came that Jonathan and his mother had to move out of their house in the woods, he had no idea what to expect. He would always visit his grandparents' home during the Holidays, but he couldn't imagine how different things would be once he moved in. The house was old, the oldest house on the entire street. It used to be a part of a giant barn back in the 1800s. The old oak floors echoed with its history, the frames on the doorway's ways scratched by years of moving furniture and remodeling. There was something cozy yet unsettling about this house. Years went by as Jonathan and his mother lived in a small room built off from the basement. Middle school, High school, break ups, arguments, a lot of different life's experiences were caged in that room. Nights spent in anger, sorrow, grief, and on the rare occasion sometimes joy. This house always felt like some distorted prison to him. Family has come and gone, his own grandfather passed away in the living room on one cold morning in February. No matter how many years went by, or how many times they would remodel the house still had an overwhelming sense of grief drowning out any room for improvements or change. It had been almost nineteen years since they moved into the family home. Time seemed to be going by so slow with every waking moment in the house. The freshly painted walls, new furniture and lively decorations seemed more like distractions or ways to cover up the stains made by the past. One room had always remained the same though... The root cellar.

Throughout Jonathan's childhood his whole family had stories of the root cellar. They would sometimes use it to instill fear into the children for misbehaving, idle and playful threats of making us go into the cellar if we wouldn't stop being bad kids. To the whole family it was nothing more than a fun joke passed down through the four generations that grew up in this house. His family has owned it for well over fifty years and they loved to talk about their rich and exciting memories that seemed like pure fables compared to the things Jonathan experienced. Jonathan is now on the verge of his twenty ninth birthday, and he is still in the family home. Helping his mother take care of her grandkids and managing his own life at the same time. Things seemed to be okay for a bit, as if everything was finally going in the right direction. Until the end of the day, when the lights are off, his mother has gone to bed and the children are sleeping. Jonathan spends most of his nights in that room he grew up in. Surrounding himself with collectibles and other things to constantly remind him of the childhood that was ripped away from him. No matter how many things he bought it didn't seem like these little nostalgic attachments could fill the void that was made in his chest nineteen years ago.

There were many days where Jonathan would be consumed by his thoughts. Contemplating if he would ever escape this cage that surrounds him. How easy could it be? He looks out at the tiny bit of sunlight creeping through the outside door. He imagines that he could simply run away right now, but to where? This cage is all that he has ever known. It was now May 12th, one month and one day away from his birthday. The sun was shining after the few days filled with rain and thunder had passed. There was a familiar breeze in the air, one that called to him for inspiration.

So, he sits at his computer and types away. The words fill the page as he gets lost in thought. His creativity is filling the room as the purple lights above him cast a shadow upon the room. Fans blaring in the background as the noise simply turns into a buzzing sound that rings in his ears. He has officially lost himself in this new drive for creation. That is until he hears banging noises coming from the basement behind him. Unfamiliar with the noise he calls his mother to see if it was her, but she informs him that she isn't home. She had stopped at the local bakery for some fresh bread as she does every Sunday morning. Jonathan simply assumes that maybe a neighbor is knocking on the front door, so he chooses to ignore it and continue his work. Then the banging happens again and this time he can hear something fall over. He stands up out of his chair and quickly opens the old white door behind him leading into the basement. The basement was filled with old decorations that his mother kept from the holidays, the bricks were old, and the blueish paint was starting to wear off. The rafters above him were covered in cobwebs as the air was filled with the same murky and moistened breeze that has haunted the stone floors since their creation. Jonathan looks around and notices that nothing has fallen over. Eager to return to his work he turns around and heads back to his chair.

The knocking happens again, this time directly behind him. He turns and looks to the right corner of the basement and sees the sheet of plastic covering the root cellar entrance has been torn. Confused by the sight he goes over to investigate, assuming one of the cats must have made its way down into the basement and simply tore the screen while exploring. As he approaches the old, dusty plastic sheet Jonathan hears scratching inside the root cellar. Worried that one of the cats might be in there and get hurt Jonathan rushes in. The Root Cellar is dark and has a dirt hill on the right side of the room. The left side of the room leads underneath the foundation of the house. There were small wooden shelves on the wall that had dusty glass jars on them. The smell of dirt and water filled the air as Jonathan was brushing the cobwebs and moving small boxes to look for the cats. One of the jars still had old vegetables in them, he opened the jar, and the odd rotting smell quickly invaded his nose. It didn't smell like the typical stench that you would experience picking up rotting food though which left Jonathan baffled but he had to continue looking for the cats

As the search continues there is scratching coming from the dirt pile behind him. Jonathan turns around quickly to see nothing but dirt and rocks falling from the hill as the plastic sheet goes flying up. Maybe the cats simply ran out of the room. Exhausted yet relieved Jonathan is making his way out of the room then more dirt starts to fall. He turns around and there is a root peeking out of the base of the hill. "There was no way that they still had vegetables down here, right?" He says to himself as he proceeds to investigate.

Jonathan reaches down to the root and goes to pull out his cellphone so he can use the flashlight. A box falls on him and knocks his phone across the room, he panics to search for it as the room gets darker by the second. He gets up to move but then feels something wrap around his ankle. The root is now traveling up his leg and has put him in a vice-like grip. Before he even gets the chance to run or scream the roots pull him into the dirt pile. He proceeds to fall for what feels like an eternity before he finally hits the ground. He gets up and looks around the room, every inch and every corner are covered in roots. The smell of rot and decay mutter through the brisk winds as the insects crawl on the floor. His cellphone starts to vibrate behind him, and he runs over to pick it up. Jonathan answers the call from an unknown number.

"Hello?" Jonathan hesitates.

The sound of a hundred voices pierces his ears as they cry out in pain. He falls to the floor as blood comes out of his ears and pours onto the ground. He looks up as the roof starts to shake and rumble. There is a giant face made of roots hanging from the ceiling. Distorted features with insects crawling in and out of it's mouth and eyes. The roots slither around the room as it starts glowing red. Jonathan sees the faces of his uncles, aunt, and grandparents wrapped into the foundation of this monstrosity. He lets out a bellowing scream as the creature slams its tentacle like roots into his throat. It lifts Jonathan up off the ground and slowly brings him into the wall. With every move Jonathan is becoming one with the roots. His mind is filled with hundreds of years of memories as his body is being mutilated. He will forever be entombed by the one cage he was so eager to escape from. Surrounded by the painful memories that have haunted him for years. His eyes fade to black as the world around him starts to crumble. The creature lets out a hateful scream as the winds tear through the room and Jonathan's life simply fades into the void.

Jonathan then takes a deep breath and wakes up. Screaming at the top of his lungs his mother cradles him. His sisters come running in to check on him. After he calms down his mom makes him his usual breakfast. Eggs and bacon while he proceeded through his morning routine. He turns on the shower, ready to relax after what seemed to be one of the worst nightmares he has ever experienced. Was it all a dream? The ninteen years he thought he experienced simply seemed like a distant memory.

As he turns on the shower and moves the curtain back, he is eager to feel the warmth of the shower. The water starts to gurgle and turn black, confused Jonathan tries to turn off the water but it keeps flowing and filling up the bathtub until it soaks the floor. The room is starting to flood to the top; Jonathan struggles to get to the bathroom door as he grabs for the doorknob. He kicks and screams begging for his family to come save him. The black liquid fills his lungs as he fades away.

Jonathan's mother comes home and yells for him to help her get stuff from the car. After he doesn't answer her a few times she gets concerned and goes down to his room. Jonathan is nowhere to be found. She goes into the basement and sees the plastic sheet in the floor then proceeds down the hallway to the root cellar. There she finds Jonathan, cold and lifeless on the floor. His hands and feet covered in dirt; lips blue from the lack of oxygen. She screeches in pain at the sight of her son's body on the floor, not realizing that the child she once knew had already died a long time ago.

Thank you so much for checking out this collection of short stories. Most of the stories featured in this book were completely left as they were originally written so that I could keep a reminder of my progress and how different my life was during each and every one of them. I have so many people that I could mention that helped motivate me to finally finish this project. To all my friends and some family, even to those of you that simply picked up the book and gave my work a chance...

Thank you.

Thank you for believing in me, thank you for supporting me, thank you for going on this journey with me, and thank you for never letting me give up on my dreams. Let this book be the final chapter of my 20's, but also the beginning of something new.

- R.J. Fester

Text © R.J. Fester
LIBRARY OF CONGRESS CATALOGING-IN-PUBLICATION
DATA Name: R.J. Fester, Author
Title: The Root Cellar
Identifiers: ASIN: B0F9NWFM6H

Printed in Great Britain
by Amazon